Toot & Puddle
You Are My Sunshine

by
Holly Hobbie

Little, Brown and Company
Boston   New York   London

First Travel Edition

Library of Congress Cataloging-in-Publication Data

Hobbie, Holly.
    Toot and Puddle : you are my sunshine / by Holly Hobbie. — 1st ed.
        p.   cm.
    Summary: Puddle cannot make his friend Toot stop moping until a huge
thunderstorm clears the air.
    ISBN 0-316-36562-9 (hc) / ISBN 0-316-14565-3 (travel)
    [1. Pigs — Fiction.   2. Friendship — Fiction.   3. Emotions — Fiction.
4. Thunderstorms — Fiction.   5. Storms — Fiction.]   I. Title.
PZ7.H6517Toe   1999
[E] — DC21   98-3665

                        HC: 10 9 8 7 6 5 4 3 2 1
                        TR: 10 9 8 7 6 5 4 3 2 1

                                    SC

                        Printed in Hong Kong

    The paintings for this book were done in watercolor.
    The text was set in Optima, and the display type is Windsor Light.

To my Mother and Father

It was morning in Woodcock Pocket. The sun was shining, birds were singing, blossoms were bursting . . .

and Toot was moping.

When Puddle asked, "What's the matter?" Toot said, "Oh, nothing."

"I've never seen Toot mope," said Tulip. "He's always so happy."

"Everybody mopes sometimes," said Puddle. "Even Toot."

"And it's such a beautiful day," Tulip said. "The sky is so blue."

"That doesn't matter when you're blue, too," Puddle said.

The next morning when Toot came into the kitchen, he asked
Puddle, "How do I look?"

"How do you look?" Puddle said. "You look the same as ever."

"My ears are too big," Toot said.

"Of course they aren't," Puddle said. "Your ears are perfect."

"Do you think my eyes are too small?" Toot asked.

Puddle looked at his friend's eyes. "I don't think so," he said.

"I feel too pink," Toot said.

"You can't be too pink."

"You're just saying that," said Toot. And he moped out of the room.

Mope

Mope

Mope

That evening Puddle made five-berry cobbler with heaps of whipped cream.

"I know five-berry cobbler is your favorite," he said to his friend.

"It's delicious," Toot told him. "Thank you." Toot's smile popped out for the first time in two days.

"It worked," Tulip sang the next
morning. "Hooray for
five-berry cobbler!"
"I think you're right," cheered
Puddle. He was very
relieved.

But when Toot came poking across the
yard, he didn't look any happier than
he had been before.

"Is Toot still blue?" Tulip asked.
"Maybe he's bored," Puddle
declared. "What Toot needs is
adventure."

"That was *tons* of adventure," Tulip said.

"We never would have dared the rapids without you," Puddle told Toot.

"Anyone can float down a river," Toot replied. He was *still* moping.

So Puddle had another idea. "Maybe Toot is feeling lonely. We haven't had company at Woodcock Pocket all summer." Tulip's eyes brightened. "There's nothing better than company," she said.

"Let's invite everyone."

Everyone came.

Ginny   Otto   Phil

Soon Puddle had everyone singing.

"Let's play hide-and-seek," Otto suggested.
"Come on, Toot," Puddle called. "You're it!"

But Toot said, "I'm not in the mood to be *it* right now."

"I think everyone had a wonderful time," Puddle said.
"Everyone but Toot," said Tulip.
"I sure miss the old Toot," Puddle said.
"Me, too," said Tulip.

Sunday morning wasn't sunny.
"I think something is coming," Puddle said anxiously.
"I'm afraid you're right," said Tulip.

Late that afternoon, lightning crackled, thunder rumbled, and wind lashed Woodcock Pocket with rain.
It was the biggest and scariest storm Puddle could remember, and it went on all night.
Toot was the only one who didn't seem afraid.

In the morning, Pocket Pond was flooded, and there were leaves and branches all over the place. But the air felt different, more fresh and exciting, and the world seemed crisp and new.

And when Toot came marching across the yard, he was the old Toot. His walk was bouncy, his head was up, and his whole pink face was smiling.

"I'm glad you're not moping anymore," Puddle said.
"Was I *moping?*" Toot asked.
"Just a little," Puddle told him. "Sometimes you need a big whopping thunderstorm to clear the air."
"Yes," said Tulip, "thunderstorms are absolutely necessary."
Friends, too, thought Toot.